A Note to Parents

Welcome to REAL KIDS READERS, a series of phonics-based books for children who are beginning to read. In the class-room, educators use phonics to teach children how to sound out unfamiliar words, providing a firm foundation for reading skills. At home, you can use REAL KIDS READERS to reinforce and build on that foundation, because the books follow the same basic phonic guidelines that children learn in school.

Of course the best way to help your child become a good reader is to make the experience fun—and REAL KIDS READERS do that, too. With their realistic story lines and lively characters, the books engage children's imaginations. With their clean design and sparkling photographs, they provide picture clues that help new readers decipher the text. The combination is sure to enter-tain young children and make them truly want to read.

REAL KIDS READERS have been developed at three distinct levels to make it easy for children to read at their own pace.

- LEVEL 1 is for children who are just beginning to read.
- LEVEL 2 is for children who can read with help.
- LEVEL 3 is for children who can read on their own.

A controlled vocabulary provides the framework at each level. Repetition, rhyme, and humor help increase word skills. Because children can understand the words and follow the stories, they quickly develop confidence. They go back to each book again and again, increasing their proficiency and sense of accomplishment, until they're ready to move on to the next level. The result is a rich and rewarding experience that will help them develop a lifelong love of reading.

For Margaret, Larry, and Jacob Pine, whose
friendship, support, and hospitality have made
my life as a writer possible. Thank you!
—K. M.

Special thanks to The Gap, Giesswein, Lisa Shaub, Marika Hahn
for Natalie & Friends, and Sara's Prints for providing clothing
and to Shoofly, New York City, for providing shoes.

Produced by DWAI / Seventeenth Street Productions, Inc.
Reading Specialist: Virginia Grant Clammer

Library of Congress Cataloging-in-Publication Data
Morris, Kimberly.
  Molly in the middle / Kimberly Morris ; photographs by Dorothy Handelman.
        p.   cm. — (Real kids readers. Level 3)
  Summary: Tired of being the middle child, Molly tries to distinguish herself from her sisters.
  ISBN 0-7613-2059-8 (lib. bdg.). — ISBN 0-7613-2084-9 (pbk.)
  [1. Birth order—Fiction. 2. Sisters—Fiction.] I. Handelman, Dorothy, ill.
II. Title. III. Series.
PZ7.M7881635Mo   1999
[E]—dc21   98-34281
                                                                    CIP
                                                                    AC

pbk: 10 9 8 7 6 5 4 3 2
lib: 10 9 8 7 6 5 4 3

Molly in the Middle

By Kimberly Morris

Photographs by Dorothy Handelman

M

The Millbrook Press

Brookfield, Connecticut

My name is Molly Muller. That's me in the middle, the one who's not smiling. The girl on the left is my sister Tina. Tina is the oldest. The girl on the right is my other sister, Lucy. Lucy is the youngest.

So here's my question. If Tina is the oldest and Lucy is the youngest, what does that make me—the *middle-est?*

I can't be the *middle-est*. I looked it up, and there's no such word! Now do you see my problem?

I'm not the oldest, and I'm not the youngest. I'm just Molly in the middle. There's nothing special about me at all.

Some new people moved in next door. When they came over to meet us, Dad said, "This is Tina. She's our oldest."

Tina said hello and shook hands with them. Nobody had to poke her in the ribs to remind her.

The new people said, "My! She's *sooooo* grown-up!"

Then Dad said, "This is Molly. She's in the middle."

As I said, there's nothing special about being in the middle. So I thought, "If I can't be the oldest and I can't be the youngest—maybe I can be the *cutest*."

I stuck *both* my thumbs in my mouth. But nobody said, *"Awwwww!"* Dad just gave me a dirty look and said, "Stop that, Molly. Your hands are full of germs."

(I guess baby thumbs don't have germs.)

When the new neighbors left, I wished I could leave too. Being stuck in the middle STINKS!

I'd rather be stuck on a leaky raft in shark-filled waters than stuck in the middle. I'd rather be stuck in a deep hole full of big snakes than stuck in the middle. I'd rather be stuck on top of the Empire State Building in a snowstorm with nothing to eat but lima beans than stuck in the middle.

15

If I were stuck on a raft, or in a hole, or on top of the Empire State Building, someone might pay attention. But when you're stuck in the middle of a family, no one really sees you.

"Okay," I thought. "If I can't be the oldest, and I can't be the youngest, and I can't be the cutest—I'll be the *loudest*. Then people will *have* to pay attention."

During dinner I yelled, "PASS THE ROLLS, PLEASE!"

Mom was so surprised, she dropped the whole basket on the floor.

Then the phone rang, and I picked it up and yelled, "HELLO! THIS IS MOLLY MULLER SPEAKING! CAN YOU HEAR ME?"

The caller had the wrong number. But now at least one person in the world knows that Molly Muller is a really loud kid.

When I went to bed that night, I yelled, "GOOD NIGHT, LUCY!"

Too bad Lucy was already asleep. She woke up, and Mom and Dad got mad and told me to stop yelling.

So then I thought, "If I can't be the oldest, and I can't be the youngest, and I can't be the cutest, and I can't be the loudest—maybe I can be the *funniest*."

The next morning, I dressed up like a clown and went downstairs to breakfast.

Lucy and Tina laughed really hard when they saw me.

"Knock! Knock!" I said.

"Who's there?" Tina asked.

"Molly," I said.

"Molly who?" Lucy asked.

Before I could answer, Dad told me to take off his good shoes. Mom told me to wash my face and stay out of her makeup.

"Wait," said Tina. "You didn't finish the joke. Molly who?"

"That's what I'm trying to find out," I said. Then I stomped out of the kitchen.

23

Now I was mad. And when I get mad, I get mean. So I thought, "That's it! If I can't be the oldest, and I can't be the youngest, and I can't be the cutest, and I can't be the loudest, and I can't be the funniest—I'll just have to be the *meanest.*"

I got all the dirty, smelly socks out of the hamper.

Then I let Lucy and Tina have it.
"HERE COMES MOLLY, THE
MEANEST MULLER OF THEM ALL!"
I yelled.

Tina tried to run away, but I got her—right in the face.

"Gross!" she screamed.

Lucy sat down on the floor and started to cry. (She's such a baby!)

28

It was wild, let me tell you, and it sure got Mom and Dad to see me. But what they saw was that I needed a time-out.

Oops!

While I was in time-out, all I could think about was how Tina and Lucy get the best deal in this family.

Did I mention that Tina gets her own room because she's the oldest? Sure, she lets me come in and play with her stuff. But it's still *her* room.

I have to share a room with Lucy.

When you're the youngest, you don't get your own room. You just get your way all the time—every single minute of every single day.

If I play with Lucy, I have to play the game *she* likes. That's because it's the only game she knows how to play! And if I argue or make a fuss, Mom tells *me* not to act like a baby.

When I thought about how unfair it all was, I wanted to stamp my feet. So I did. BAM! BAM! BAM! I stamped so hard, the floor shook. That's when Dad came into the room and asked me what was wrong.

"What's wrong is that I'm stuck in the middle," I told him. "I'm too young to have my own room. But I'm too old to act like a baby. I can't yell. Nobody thinks I'm funny. I'm not allowed to be mean. And on top of everything else, MY THUMBS ARE FULL OF COOTIES!"

"I see your problem," Dad said. "So just for today, you can be the youngest or the oldest. Which would you like to be?"

"I want to be the oldest—so I can have my own room," I said.

"You won't mind sleeping by yourself?" Dad asked.

He had a point. I *would* mind sleeping in a room by myself. In fact, I'd be scared.

"I changed my mind," I said. "I'll be the youngest."

"Then your bedtime will be an hour earlier," Dad told me. "Oh, and don't forget. You're not allowed in Tina's room, and you can't play with her things anymore."

"Why not?" I said.

"Because you're too young," Dad said. "You leave sticky fingerprints on books. You lose puzzle pieces."

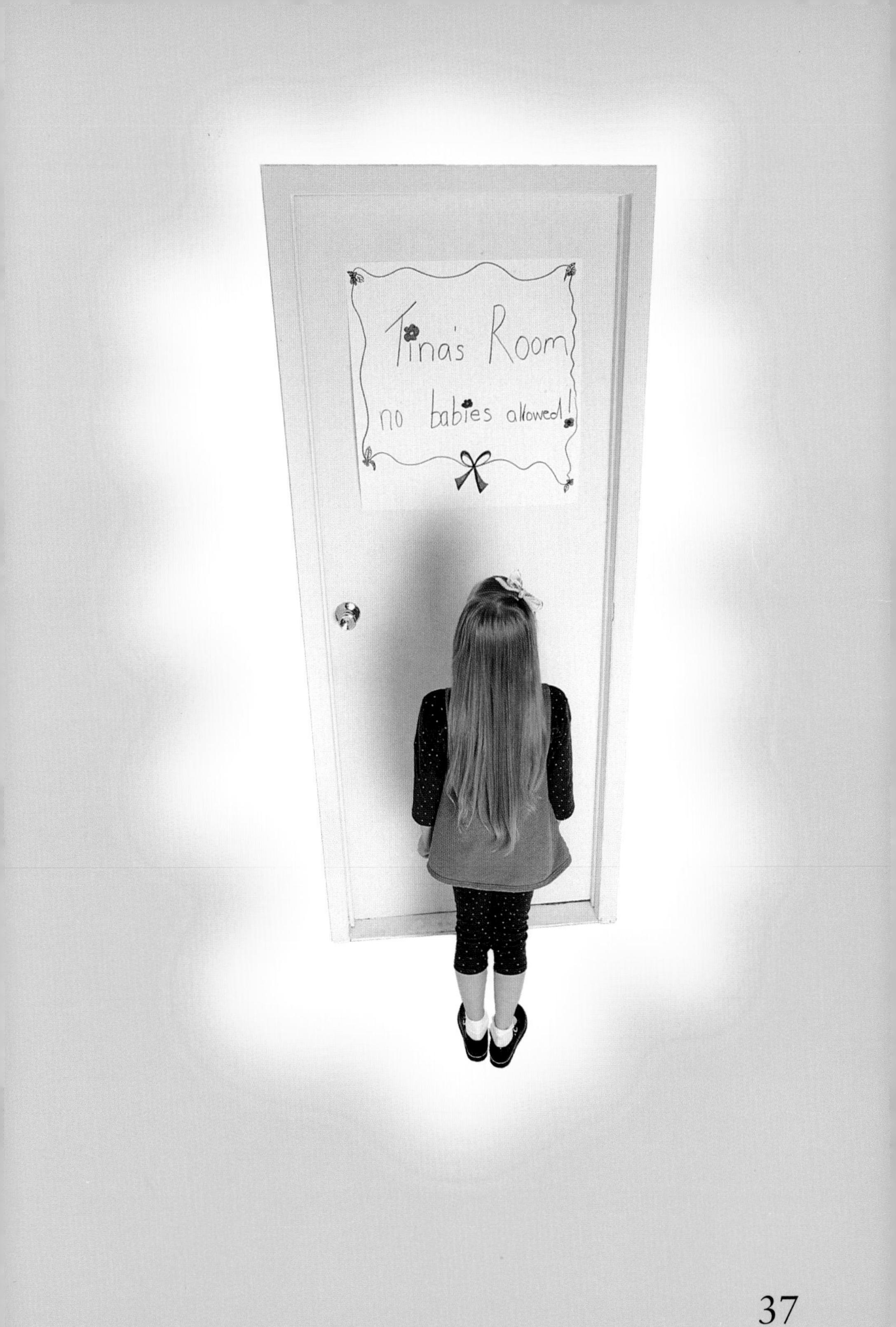
Tina's Room
no babies allowed!

"I changed my mind again," I said. "I want to be the oldest."

Dad smiled. "Then I want you to play with Lucy for an hour. Mom and I are going to work in the yard. We need you to watch her."

"How can I play with Lucy for a whole hour?" I said. "She only knows one stupid baby game."

Dad whispered in my ear so Lucy couldn't hear him. "Pretend you like it—and let her win. You're the oldest, remember. You're much too grown-up to beat a baby at a baby game."

"Let me think it over," I said.

Dad left and I thought some more. Maybe being in the middle wasn't so bad after all. Maybe *I* was the one who had the best deal.

I made a list of the good things about being in the middle. Here's what I wrote.

1. I'm old enough to stay up as late as Tina.

2. I'm old enough to play with her stuff, but I don't have to sleep by myself.

3. Nobody expects me to remember to shake hands.

4. I don't have to watch Lucy when Mom and Dad are busy.

5. I'm not too old to play with Lucy if I feel like it.

6. I actually _like_ that baby game. I like it because it's easy and I always win!

After I read over my list, I felt better. Then I thought, "Maybe sometime, if I'm feeling grown-up, I'll let Lucy win. Or I'll help her do one of Tina's puzzles and make sure she doesn't lose the pieces. But only if I *want* to. I don't *have* to. Mom and Dad don't *expect* me to."

1. I'm old enough to stay up as late as Tina.

2. I'm old enough to play with her stuff, but I don't have to sleep by myself.

3. Nobody expects me to remember to shake hands.

4. I don't have to watch Lucy when Mom and Dad are busy.

5. I'm not too old to play with l. if I feel like it.

6. I actually

43

A little while later, Dad came back. "Well?" he said. "What did you decide?"

"I'm staying in the middle," I said. Then I jumped up and got my jacket.

"Where are you going?" Dad asked.

"I'm going next door," I said. "I want to tell the new people that I'm not the oldest, and I'm not the youngest, and I'm not the cutest, and I'm not the loudest, and I'm not the funniest, and I'm not the meanest. I'm Molly in the middle.

"And that makes me the *luckiest!*"

Reading with Your Child

Even though your child is reading more independently now, it is vital that you continue to take part in this important learning experience.

- Try to read with your child at least twenty minutes each day, as part of your regular routine.
- Encourage your child to keep favorite books in one convenient, cozy spot, so you don't waste valuable reading time looking for them.
- Read and familiarize yourself with the Phonic Guidelines on the next pages.
- Praise your young reader. Be the cheerleader, not the teacher. Your enthusiasm and encouragement are key ingredients in your child's success.

What to Do if Your Child Gets Stuck on a Word

- Wait a moment to see if he or she works it out alone.
- Help him or her decode the word phonetically. Say, "Try to sound it out."
- Encourage him or her to use picture clues. Say, "What does the picture show?"
- Encourage him or her to use context clues. Say, "What would make sense?"
- Ask him or her to try again. Say, "Read the sentence again and start the tricky word. Get your mouth ready to say it."
- If your child still doesn't "get" the word, tell him or her what it is. Don't wait for frustration to build.

What to Do if Your Child Makes a Mistake

- If the mistake makes sense, ignore it—unless it is part of a pattern of errors you wish to correct.
- If the mistake doesn't make sense, wait a moment to see if your child corrects it.
- If your child doesn't correct the mistake, ask him or her to try again, either by decoding the word or by using context or picture clues. Say, "Get your mouth ready" or "Make it sound right" or "Make it make sense."
- If your child still doesn't "get" the word, tell him or her what it is. Don't wait for frustration to build.

Phonic Guidelines

Use the following guidelines to help your child read the words in this story.

Short Vowels
When two consonants surround a vowel, the sound of the vowel is usually short. This means you pronounce *a* as in apple, *e* as in egg, *i* as in igloo, *o* as in octopus, and *u* as in umbrella. Words with short vowels include: *bed, big, box, cat, cup, dad, dog, get, hid, hop, hum, jam, kid, mad, met, mom, pen, ran, sad, sit, sun, top.*

R-Controlled Vowels
When a vowel is followed by the letter *r*, its sound is changed by the *r*. Words with *r*-controlled vowels include: *card, curl, dirt, farm, girl, herd, horn, jerk, torn, turn.*

Long Vowel and Silent E
If a word has a vowel followed by a consonant and an *e*, usually the vowel is long and the *e* is silent. Long vowels are pronounced the same way as their alphabet names. Words with a long vowel and silent *e* include: *bake, cute, dive, game, home, kite, mule, page, pole, ride, vote.*

Double Vowels
When two vowels are side by side, usually the first vowel is long and the second vowel is silent. Words with double vowels include: *boat, clean, gray, loaf, meet, neat, paint, pie, play, rain, sleep, tried.*

Diphthongs
Sometimes when two vowels (or a vowel and a consonant) are side by side, they combine to make a diphthong—a sound that is different from long or short vowel sounds. Diphthongs are: *au/aw, ew, oi/oy, ou/ow.* Words with diphthongs include: *auto, brown, claw, flew, found, join, toy.*

Double Consonants
When two identical consonants appear side by side, one of them is silent. Words with double consonants include: *bell, fuss, mess, mitt, puff, tall, yell.*

Consonant Blends
When two or more different consonants are side by side, they usually blend to make a combined sound. Words with consonant blends include: *bent, blob, bride, club, crib, drop, flip, frog, gift, glare, grip, help, jump, mask, most, pink, plane, ring, send, skate, sled, spin, steep, swim, trap, twin.*

Consonant Digraphs

Sometimes when two different consonants are side by side, they make a digraph that represents a single new sound. Consonant digraphs are: *ch, sh, th, wh*. Words with digraphs include: *bath, chest, lunch, sheet, think, whip, wish*.

Silent Consonants

Sometimes, when two different consonants are side by side, one of them is silent. Words with silent consonants include: *back, dumb, knit, knot, lamb, sock, walk, wrap, wreck*.

Sight Words

Sight words are those words that a reader must learn to recognize immediately—by sight—instead of by sounding them out. They occur with high frequency in easy texts. Sight words include: *a, am, an, and, as, at, be, big, but, can, come, do, for, get, give, have, he, her, his, I, in, is, it, just, like, look, make, my, new, no, not, now, old, one, out, play, put, red, run, said, see, she, so, some, soon, that, the, then, there, they, to, too, two, under, up, us, very, want, was, we, went, what, when, where, with, you*.

Exceptions to the "Rules"

Although much of the English language is phonically regular, there are many words that don't follow the above guidelines. For example, a particular combination of letters can represent more than one sound. Double *oo* can represent a long *oo* sound, as in words such as *boot, cool,* and *moon;* or it can represent a short *oo* sound, as in words such as *foot, good,* and *hook*. The letters *ow* can represent a diphthong, as in words such as *brow, fowl,* and *town;* or they can represent a long *o* sound, as in words such as *blow, snow,* and *tow*. Additionally, some high-frequency words such as *some, come, have,* and *said* do not follow the guidelines at all, and *ough* appears in such different-sounding words as *although, enough,* and *thought*.

The phonic guidelines provided in this book are just that—guidelines. They do not cover all the irregularities in our rich and varied language, but are intended to correspond roughly to the phonic lessons taught in the first and second grades. Phonics provides the foundation for learning to read. Repetition, visual clues, context, and sheer experience provide the rest.